Thomas Nelson and Sons Ltd
Nelson House Mayfield Road
Walton-on-Thames Surrey
KT12 5PL UK

51 York Place
Edinburgh
EH1 3JD UK

Thomas Nelson (Hong Kong) Ltd
Toppan Building 10/F
22A Westlands Road
Quarry Bay Hong Kong

Thomas Nelson Australia
102 Dodds Street
South Melbourne
Victoria 3205
Australia

Nelson Canada
1120 Birchmount Road
Scarborough Ontario
M1K 5G4   Canada

© Templar Publishing Ltd 1985
First published by Hamlyn Publishing 1985
Second and subsequent impressions published by Thomas Nelson & Sons Ltd from 1989

Letterland was devised by Lyn Wendon and is part of
the *Pictogram* system © Lyn Wendon 1973-1986

ISBN 0-17-410151-1
NPN 9

Printed in Italy

Bouncy Ben's Birthday

Written by Richard Carlisle
Illustrated by Jane Launchbury

Nelson

Bouncy Ben was so excited. Tomorrow was his birthday. Tucked under his blanket that night, he could hardly sleep.

He lay awake thinking of all the presents he wanted. If only he could have a new bat and ball!

He tried to imagine what other surprises might be waiting for him when he woke up.

N ext morning Bouncy Ben bounded out of bed and was down to breakfast in a flash.

His brothers were already at the breakfast table munching bread and butter.

"You look bright-eyed and bushy-tailed this morning," they said. "That's because today is a special day!" said Bouncy Ben brightly.

He started to look around for his presents, but he could not see a single one. He looked underneath the table. There were none there either.

Bouncy Ben was bewildered.
He finished his breakfast and
bounced outside.
There were no presents outside,
not even under the bushes.

His brothers began playing ball near
the bridge. Bouncy Ben hopped over
to them.

"Aren't you going to wish me Happy
B..?" Bouncy Ben started to say.
But his brothers just kept on playing.
They didn't seem to be listening.

Bouncy Ben sat by the bridge watching his brothers.
He was beginning to feel very sorry for himself. No-one seemed to have remembered his birthday!

He even sneaked another look behind some bushes to see if his presents were hidden there. But the bushes were bare.

Soon Ben's brothers had finished their game. They decided to go for a walk into the woods.

"Can I come, too?" asked Ben.
"If you really want to,"
said his brothers as they bounced along the path that led into the woods.

Bouncy Ben hopped along behind them rather slowly. Soon he was far behind. His brothers were nearly out of sight.

Bouncy Ben stopped and ate some berries. That made him feel a little better. Then he bounded ahead, expecting to see his brothers waiting for him ... but they weren't.

He wasn't even sure which way they went. Ben was beginning to think he was lost.

Suddenly, he heard the sound of singing. It came from the other side of some bushes.
Ben raced towards the sound, until he could hear the words.

He burst through the bushes.
All his brothers were there!
They had been waiting for him…
and they were singing…

"**H**appy birthday, to you.
Happy birthday, to you.
Happy birthday dear Ben,
Happy birthday to you!"
they sang happily.

"You have remembered my birthday!"
shouted Ben, as he bounced into the
air with joy.

His brothers were standing by a
beautiful birthday cake with bright
blue candles. There were lots of
presents too, all neatly tied up with
big, blue ribbons.

ouncy Ben could hardly wait to open his presents. All his brothers watched as he opened the first one. Inside was a new ball!

Then he opened the second present.
Inside was a brand new bat.
Just what he wanted.

Bouncy Ben beamed.

Bouncy Ben's brothers smiled too. They had another surprise for him.

"Time to play 'Blind Man's Buff'," said his brothers. They put a blindfold over his eyes and led him into a field.

"Now catch us," they cried.

Bouncy Ben tried to catch them. Instead he caught …. a big, big basket!

"It's your birthday treat!"
cried his brothers, pulling off
Ben's blindfold.
"A balloon ride."
"Oh, how beautiful!" Ben shouted.
"Let's all jump into the basket."

So Bouncy Ben and his brothers all
bounced into the basket.

Up, up and away went the balloon.

Then Ben saw lots of other beautiful balloons floating up. They rose higher and higher until Ben saw that they had letters on them. He read the words they made.

'Happy Birthday, Ben', they said.

Everyone in Letterland had remembered that today was his birthday!

"What a day!" cried Ben.
"The best birthday ever!"

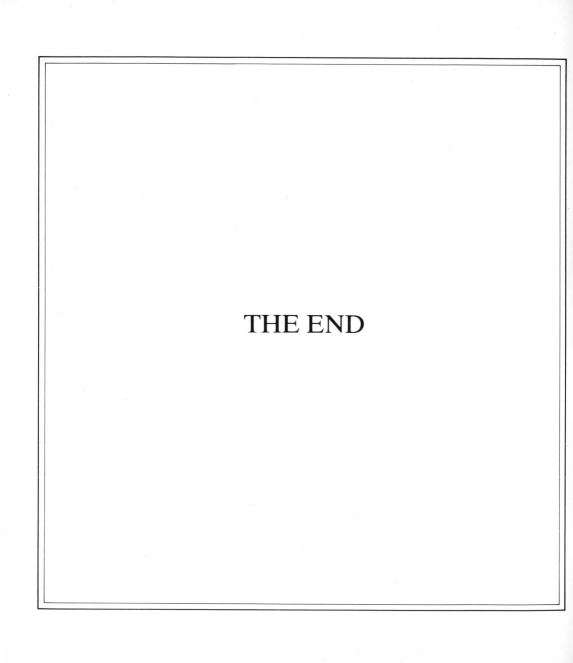

THE END